BILLBOARD EXPRESS

Sigmund Brouwer
& Cindy Morgan

ORCA BOOK PUBLISHERS

Library and Archives Canada Cataloguing in Publication

Brouwer, Sigmund, 1959–, author
Billboard express / Sigmund Brouwer & Cindy Morgan.
(Orca limelights)

Issued in print and electronic formats.
ISBN 978-1-4598-1108-9 (paperback).—ISBN 978-1-4598-1109-6 (pdf).—
ISBN 978-1-4598-1110-2 (epub)

I. Morgan, Cindy, 1968–, author II. Title. III. Series: Orca limelights
PS8553.R68467B55 2016   jC813'.54   C2016-900542-9
C2016-900543-7

First published in the United States, 2016
Library of Congress Control Number: 2016933645

Summary: This high-interest novel for teen readers is set in Nashville,
where Elle, a talented musician, tries to make it in the cutthroat music business.

*Orca Book Publishers is dedicated to preserving the environment and has printed
this book on Forest Stewardship Council® certified paper.*

Orca Book Publishers gratefully acknowledges the support for
its publishing programs provided by the following agencies:
the Government of Canada through the Canada Book Fund and the Canada
Council for the Arts, and the Province of British Columbia through the BC
Arts Council and the Book Publishing Tax Credit.

Cover design by Rachel Page
Cover photography by iStock.com

ORCA BOOK PUBLISHERS
www.orcabook.com

Printed and bound in Canada.

19 18 17 16 • 4 3 2 1

To those who feel the undeniable call of the arts.
Let your light shine.
Be true to the light and to yourself.

One

"Got a mirror or something?" Elle's manager, Bernie, asked as they stepped out of the elevator for their meeting with the label execs. Execs, not executives. Bernie said it was important to know the lingo.

Elle was holding a guitar case, switching hands frequently to keep the guitar between her and Bernie. Like a shield.

He pointed at Elle's hair. "Must have been the wind out there. You've got a few wild strands on the left side, and that black stuff is clumped a little on your eyes. Mascara or eyeliner? Either way, you need to fix it."

"Bernie," Elle said. "My hair doesn't sing. Or play guitar."

Elle tried not to inhale the smell of Bernie's mouthwash. He was a close talker, always inside her personal space. That was bad enough, but Bernie qualified for senior-citizen discounts and looked like the creepy kind of guy who hung out in the lingerie section of Walmart. The smell of that mouthwash was laced with the whiff of booze. Ten thirty in the morning and Bernie had already had a little more than cream in his coffee. Apparently it was more important to know the lingo than to wait until the end of the workday to have a few shots of whiskey.

"Huh?" Bernie said.

Elle knew it would be juvenile to snap out a snarky comment about how at least she had hair that the wind could move around. Bernie's thinning hair was greased down and combed sideways, probably capable of withstanding a hurricane. Yet somehow he managed to have flakes of dandruff on his black shirt with the over-size collar, a shirt from a time when cell phones were the size of toasters.

Yeah. Juvenile. And far too easy. Much better to focus her snark on his lack of intelligence. How this guy could possibly be one of the best country music managers in the business was a mystery to Elle. She hoped she'd learn the answer at her first real meeting with the label execs.

"You heard me," Elle said. "Hair can't sing. Or play guitar. So I'll sing and play and let my hair take a break from all that work."

Bernie blinked a few times, absorbing her words, then lifted his arm. His shiny, cheap suit crinkled as he reached into a pocket, pulled out an envelope and handed it to Elle.

She opened it and recognized her father's handwriting on the letter inside.

Trust him and follow every order, the note said. *Bernie's been in the biz for years, and word has it he's got the connections to make things happen. For what he's costing us on retainer, I don't need you to second-guess what he does.*

"Daddy told me you had an attitude," Bernie said, "which is why he gave me the note. Daddy also signs the checks. And I've already been paid enough that I can walk right now and it won't bother me. Want to do it his way, which is also my way? Or want to go into that meeting alone while I go spend Daddy's money?"

It was Elle's turn to blink. Her first label had folded early in the year, and in the weeks since then, she'd been in Nashville, looking for a new deal. And she was beginning to learn that talent alone wasn't enough. Also, if she walked, she'd have to explain that to her father, and that wouldn't be pretty.

On the other hand, if she did it Bernie's way, she'd essentially become his puppet. Elle wasn't about to let that happen. Not a chance.

"Go ahead, Bernie," Elle said. "I'll do this meeting myself and tell them that you stopped along the way to drink more whiskey. While you're enjoying my daddy's money, think about how much more you could have made by hanging around."

Elle headed down the hallway, holding her breath. She hated that she needed Bernie, but it felt good, leaving him there.

Two

Bernie caught up to her a few steps later.

"Come on," he said. "You need to fix that hair. How you look is a big deal in this biz."

Elle's anger began to settle. He couldn't be blamed for how she reacted when people tried to push her around.

"Bernie," Elle said, "didn't anyone ever teach you to say please? Makes things a lot smoother."

"Sure," he said. "I like that. Now about your hair."

He must have correctly understood the look that crossed her face. "Could you please fix it?" he said a moment later.

"I'd be happy to do it," Elle said.

Bernie let out a loud sigh, as if he was having second thoughts about chasing her down the hallway.

She almost said something about his sigh but decided she had already won this round. So she set down her guitar case, found a mirror in her tiny purse, searched for the stray hairs and smoothed them into place. Then she examined her eye makeup. The wind had made her eyes water, and her mascara had run. A quick swipe with a Q-tip took care of that.

As they walked to the meeting room, she looked at all the framed gold records that lined the hall of this legendary Nashville building. This was good—better than good.

Bernie was a pain, but Elle could deal with that. She had a development deal with a great label. She also had the full financial and emotional support of her father, whose chain of lumber stores in Minnesota was the foundation of a huge financial empire. Elle had a great voice, a strong work ethic. She had come a long way from when she was Charlene Adams, an overweight girl teased by her classmates and painfully self-conscious about her weight. But she'd always had talent.

She had a snake tattoo running up the inside of her wrist. It had been a reward to herself for finally fitting into a size 8 pair of jeans. Yeah, size 8 was big compared to what most of the tiny country stars wore, but she still drew a lot of attention for her looks. Small, curvy and dark-haired. Not your average Nashville bimbo.

Yes. All the dieting and working out had been worth it. The change of name had been her first producer's idea.

She sure wasn't Charlene Adams anymore. Hadn't been for a long time. No more singing alone in her bedroom as a way to keep from crying in the lonely mansion in Minneapolis. No, she was Elle McWilliam now, and she was a few steps away from walking into a meeting with a bunch of top label execs who all had one goal.

To make her a country star.

Three

When they reached the reception desk, there was a bank of video screens lining one wall, playing music videos of recent releases from the label's biggest stars.

The receptionist had golden hair and glossy lips and a Southern drawl. She wore dark-rinse skinny jeans and a loose, sheer top over a tight cami.

Elle had heard that some girls took jobs as receptionists in hopes of getting close enough to the label execs to get a shot at playing them their own music. Some label execs, she knew, were interested in more than music. This girl looked a couple of years older than Elle—maybe nineteen or twenty—but she certainly looked the part of a country star. Hair extensions, fake tan, professionally whitened teeth.

Bernie told the receptionist they were there to meet Eddy Manus.

She picked up the phone and buzzed someone, shaking her mane of hair and smiling as she talked.

"Okay, I'll tell them," she said. "Just have a seat right over there," she said to Elle and Bernie. "Eddy will be out in a few minutes. His last meeting is running a little late."

"Typical Nashville," Bernie said to Elle. "It doesn't exactly run like clockwork."

Elle watched the videos as she waited, making a mental note that of the six videos rotating on the three screens, only one video featured a female artist. There was not, however, a lack of female presence.

All the videos featuring male country stars were buzzing with girls in halter tops and tight shorts, girls who caressed bottles of beer and danced around in truck beds and frolicked on the beach in string bikinis and cowgirl hats. Their bodies were all so perfect, they looked as if they'd been airbrushed. Elle knew it was all lighting and makeup and carefully chosen camera angles. Elle glanced down at her outfit, wondering how she would ever look as sexy as those women without also looking trashy.

There wasn't anything about trucks or beer in any of Elle's lyrics. She wrote and sang songs about wanting to be loved and accepted. Songs from her heart. She had been forced by Bernie to record one song (that she despised) about a cowgirl wanting to make a cowboy happy—by cooking him a great meal.

Ugh. So fake.

But Bernie's advice to Elle and her father was that if Elle wanted to make it in Nashville, that's what it would take.

"There y'all are." The loud Southern drawl came from a thirtysomething guy wearing worn jeans and a black button-down polo shirt. The kind that cost a hundred dollars a pop.

Elle was surprised at how casually the man was dressed. Peeking out beneath the frayed bottom of his jeans was a worn-in, very expensive pair of Tony Lama cowboy boots. His teeth were perfectly straight and blindingly white. Hair trimmed neatly and, she guessed, dyed.

He looked at Elle, holding her gaze for a moment before extending his hand. "And you must be Elle. I'm Eddy. Eddy Manus. Pleased to meet you. Y'all come on back."

This was a man who held her future in his hands. She should have been terrified, but she relied on her standard response to any threat: courage fueled by defiance. She'd show him what she could do with a guitar and her voice.

They followed Eddy into a large room with a long black table surrounded by plush, gray high-back chairs. On one side was a wall of windows with a view of the impressive Nashville skyline. You could see everything—the arena where the Preds played, the Batman building, the Country Music Hall of Fame, Union Station. Elle knew how beautiful it was at night with the city lit up. Her condo had a similar view.

On the other side of the room was a black leather bar with a fancy espresso machine and a large selection of liquor. Elle looked over and caught Bernie licking his cracked lips, probably at the thought of a little top-off for the meeting.

Two other men followed them into the room. "Boys, y'all know Bernie, of course," Eddy said. Was it Elle's imagination, or was Eddy's tone cool when he introduced Bernie?

"And this lovely little thang," Eddy continued, "is Elle. Elle, this is Tommy, our head of A&R, and this is Grant, the head of our marketing team. I thought it would be good for them to sit in on the meeting as well."

A&R. Elle knew that it stood for Artists and Repertoire. Tommy was the one who worked directly with the artists. He was shorter—and thinner—than Elle. Not a large man. Midthirties, maybe, with dark tortoiseshell geek-chic glasses framing eyes surrounded by subtle smile lines. He wore loose-fitting jeans and a brown-plaid button-down shirt. Target brand would be her guess. Much less than a hundred a pop.

Grant, the marketing guy, was younger—mid-twenties. Hair buzzed short, the way guys often styled it when they were going bald early. He was dressed just like Eddy, and that told Elle something. Grant was Eddy's guy. Tommy—not so much.

Eddy offered everyone drinks. Elle asked for a bottle of water, and Bernie asked for coffee black. Good thing, Elle thought. Unless Bernie had a flask hidden in his suit jacket.

Bernie started in about how when he first saw Elle sing at a local songwriters' night he had a feeling about her. She was something special. He rambled on about the first time he saw Trisha Yearwood back in the day, said he had that same feeling about Elle. The other men nodded as if they understood that whether they liked this guy or not, he did have a knack for picking winners.

Finally Bernie said, "But talk is talk, boys. Let's do what we really came here to do. Let's hear some music. And then you'll know why this girl is headed on a ride I like to call the *Billboard* Express."

Four

Bernie pulled out a CD and handed it to Eddy. Elle had been in Nashville long enough not to be surprised. No flash drives. No downloads from the cloud. Musical currency was still the shiny silver of a CD.

"These are just some low-budget demos," Bernie said. "Hope you'll overlook some of the production issues."

Low budget since when, she thought. Bernie had insisted her demos be produced by an A-list Nashville producer with A-list musicians. The demos were meant to dazzle a label. Radio-ready, as they said. Radio-ready did not come cheap.

Eddy walked over to a sound system and popped in the CD and turned it on. Elle watched for reactions as the three execs and Bernie listened with their eyes closed. Nodding now and again. Every time they got through a verse and a chorus, Eddy would fast-forward to the next song.

Bernie had warned Elle that it was rare for music execs to listen to whole songs. Once they got the gist, they moved on. They were smiling and nodding now, which was encouraging, but Elle knew the pressure wasn't off yet. She stared down at her guitar case, knowing the moment of truth was coming.

Bernie had intentionally put the cowboy song last on the six-song demo. He had said the "radio candy" would leave them smiling.

Elle's voice came from the speakers, backed by the silkiest session guitarists in the world.

Hey, cowboy, hang your hat on my heart and throw your boots under my bed.

This love we've got has me in over my head...

Bernie's prediction proved correct. The execs seemed very into the cowboy song, looking at each other with knowing smiles. Elle felt the first nagging of worry. She was from a small town in Minnesota, but she had been raised in an upscale neighborhood where kids drove BMWs, not horses, to her elite private school. The song was just so over-the-top and so absolutely not true to who she was as a person or a singer. They listened to the whole thing, and she was relieved when the song finally ended.

Eddy was the first to speak. "Those are some great-sounding songs, Elle. Did you write those yourself?"

The real answer was that she had worked on some of the lyrics with a Canadian guy her own age named Jim Webb, who was trying to make it in Nashville just like she was.

"Well," Elle began, thinking it would be a good time to mention his name and give him credit, "I—"

Bernie interrupted. "Eddy, you know this isn't a meeting about finding another songwriter for the label. You're looking for a star, and here she is. Right in front of you."

Elle bit back anger at the interruption. Was she not allowed to speak for herself?

Eddy laughed, and then Tommy, the A&R guy spoke up. "I notice you brought your guitar. Can you play it?"

Here it was. The moment of truth. Bernie was nodding and smiling like he knew something they didn't know. Bernie was definitely not her friend.

Tommy went on. "How about playing us something new, so we can hear what you sound like live?"

Elle nodded her head as she reached down to undo the latches on the case of her vintage 1956 Gibson LG. It was her pride and joy. She was so protective of it, her dad had insisted on buying a seat for it in first class when she flew from Minnesota to Nashville. She also loved to play her Fender electric, but the acoustic was any song-writer's prize possession.

Elle took a deep breath, and as she played the opening notes and started to sing, she got lost in the words and their meaning. It was as if her entire life had led to this moment. All the hours practicing in her room meant her fingers moved across the strings with ease. She had played this song a hundred times, and for a minute she felt like she was back in her room and not in this intimidating office, with her life's dream on the line.

She played the whole song. At the end, there was a gaping moment of silence. That could be good or bad. When she looked up, she had a feeling it was good. They all seemed speechless. Bernie was beaming.

Grant, the marketing guy, leaned forward, smiling. "Elle, I have one final question for you."

"Sure," she said.

"How would you feel about being a blond?"

Five

When her phone vibrated, it took Elle a few seconds to pull herself from sleep and orient herself.

She'd drifted to sleep on her leather couch, newly purchased and delivered to her downtown condo a few days after her arrival in Nashville a few months earlier. The lights were off in her living room. The neon lights on the street, some seven stories below, gave her barely enough light to see her phone.

Elle blinked to focus as she pulled the device toward her: 10:42 PM. The caller ID showed her father's number. As usual, he'd waited until he'd finished his standard fourteen-hour workday to call her.

"Hey," she answered. "Glad you called."

"Taking care of yourself?" he answered. Years of television commercials for his lumber stores had made his voice famous in Minnesota. He was also famous for the hokey plaid flannel shirt he wore to make it look like he was a common man, a blue-collar kind of guy who liked do-it-yourself projects. Steven Adams. Trust him. Trust his business. And ignore the fact that he flies around the country in a private jet to handle all his other business interests.

"Yes," Elle said. "Taking care of myself."

Taking care of yourself was Steven Adams's code for not partying and making stupid decisions. To Elle, it was code for *I'll do my best not to let you down.* Someday she'd have to figure out how to get out of his shadow.

"All good with the condo?" he asked.

"Looks better than the day I moved in," she said. He always asked when he called. She couldn't figure out if it was because he was concerned about it as an investment, or if he liked reminding her that he'd put her in the heart of the Gulch, a part of Nashville where rich young professionals could pretend they were hipsters.

"Got your message," he said.

Elle pushed off the couch and moved to the big window. She could see the river skyline, a view that always reminded her she was in Nashville to chase her dreams.

"I wanted to talk to you about Bernie," she said. With her free hand she ran a fingertip down the window. "That note you gave him. Not funny."

"I wanted to talk about that too," he said. "I just spent half an hour on the phone with him."

"Hang on." Elle braced herself against the window. "Bernie goes running to you instead of talking to me?"

Her father's sigh came through very clearly. Strange, Elle thought. He was a thousand miles away, but that sigh managed to make her feel like she was five years old again. Her shoulders drooped under the weight of his disappointment.

"I'm paying him," he said. "Of course he reports to me."

"Then at least you know what I wanted to talk to you about. The label people want—"

"I know exactly what they want because Bernie told me. And Bernie also told me that you nearly blew the meeting."

"I—"

"He said he had to keep you from interrupting after they asked if you would mind being a blond."

"I—"

"Do you know how to fix your car?" he asked.

Her car was a two-seater BMW. She would have preferred a Mini Cooper. More fun. Less about her father reminding everyone that he could afford to give her a Beamer.

"No," she said. She loved her dad so much it made her ache. He also made her so angry that she wanted to scream. This, she thought, was going to be one of those moments.

"So," he continued, "when you bring it to the dealership, do you tell the mechanic what to do?"

Elle's view of the river blurred. But she wasn't going to let her father know her eyes had filled with tears of frustration.

"No," she said. She kept her hand pressed against the window. Outside was the night air. Freedom.

"Bernie's the mechanic," her father said. "He's going to make sure the engine of your career is in perfect condition."

"But they want me to be a blond," Elle said.

"And that's a big deal?"

"It's..." She let her voice trail away. If she tried to explain how little the meeting had been about her music, it would only prove what her father was telling her. Bernie was the mechanic, and she needed to stay out of his way as he tuned the engine.

"So is it a big deal?" he repeated. "I hope not. We've talked about this before. The music business is called the music business because it's a business. They sell one thing, I sell another. So is going blond a big deal?"

She knew what he expected for an answer.

"It's not a big deal," she said. She could walk away from Bernie when he was a jerk, but how could she walk away from her dad?

"You'll look great as a blond," he said. "Bernie says if that's what they want, that's what we need to give them."

"It's not a big deal," she said again, her voice sounding a little too chipper. Maybe she was trying to convince herself.

"Great," he said. "Hey, it's been a long day. I need to get some sleep."

"Me too," she said. Before hanging up, she added what he expected. "And don't worry. I'll take care of myself."

Six

Elle was lying in bed the next morning, only half awake, when her cell buzzed. She looked at the caller ID and let out a sigh.

Bernie.

He was the last person she wanted to talk to when she was still feeling so frustrated and upset with her dad. She decided to let it go to voice mail. She wasn't ready to face Bernie Comb-Over yet. She needed a shower and a chai latte before talking to anyone. Otherwise she might snap his head off.

She gave it a minute, then listened to the message Bernie had left.

"Elle, listen, I just got a call from Tommy, the A&R man from Starstruck Records. He wants to meet with you, talk over a few things. I'm about to go into a meeting, but here's his secretary's number. Give her a call and schedule the appointment. Very important! Let me know you got this message ASAP. Bye."

Elle looked for a piece of paper and scribbled down the number, but instead of calling Bernie back, she waited a few minutes and then texted to let him know she got the message.

After she showered and put on her zebra-print robe, she made a chai latte in her coffee machine and then called Tommy's secretary, Gretchen, who turned out to be really nice and easy to talk to. She asked Elle to come in at around eleven thirty that morning—Tommy wanted to take Elle to lunch.

Which led to a crucial problem. What to wear.

Elle stared at her clothes. Even though she was happy with her new size-8 body, sometimes she still struggled with her former body-image issues. She had always been pretty, but never thin. Now she felt confident in her new clothes, but she still had to remind herself that although she was still curvy, she wasn't the chubby little girl she used to be.

She chose a pair of light-wash skinny jeans with brown suede, open-toed shoe boots, a simple white

T-shirt and a long lightweight tan sweater with tassels at the bottom. The tee was short enough to accentuate her waist without showing any skin.

She knew she was probably more modest than most girls her age, but that's how things were done in Minnesota. *Show class, not trash,* her mother always said.

Elle missed her mom, who had died of breast cancer when Elle was going into grade ten. She closed her eyes and breathed deeply. Sometimes, like now, the memories would hit unexpectedly, and it would seem as if her mother had died the day before.

She willed herself not to cry. She didn't want to have to redo her makeup.

* * *

When she reached the desk with the bank of video screens in the Starstruck offices, the receptionist immediately looked up.

"Hey there, let me buzz Tommy. He's expecting you." The Southern drawl was so deep, Elle wondered if the receptionist faked it. Some men, apparently, loved that kind of accent.

A few minutes later, Elle and Tommy were walking down 16th Avenue, also known as Music Row. Tommy told her a bit of history about the great artists and music that had been recorded throughout the years in the hallowed buildings. He knew his stuff, and he was enthusiastic about it. Elle liked that. Tommy didn't seem as business driven as Grant did, and he obviously loved music for the sake of music.

Another thing Elle liked was Tommy's decision to get sushi. That didn't seem cowboy at all. They found an outside table, and even before the waitress could take their order, several people stopped by the table to greet Tommy, who introduced them to Elle. All were musicians and songwriters. It seemed to Elle that people genuinely liked Tommy and that he fit in more with the artistic crowd than he did with businesspeople like Eddy or Grant or Bernie. The weight of frustration she had felt when dealing with her father suddenly lifted from her shoulders. Maybe there was someone on her side. Someone who would listen.

Seven

Tommy did listen. He asked her questions about her background, the music she listened to, the books she had read. They liked some of the same musicians and movies.

He nodded his head as he listened, totally engaged, asking questions. Their conversation went much deeper than she had expected it to. She thought he would be all business, but he seemed genuinely interested in her.

When they were finished eating, Tommy took a deep breath and leaned back in his chair.

"Elle, I can tell you're smart. Thoughtful. I was impressed by the song you played in the office yesterday—just you and your guitar. It had so much heart. So much emotion. I believe that songs written from an honest and even vulnerable place are the songs that really connect with people. I think you have the ability to write those kinds of songs."

Elle knew she was blushing. She hoped her embarrassment didn't show too much. Defiance was a great way to treat a hostile world. Dealing with compliments seemed tougher to do somehow.

"You're young and green, but I see the spark of something very special in you," he continued. "That is why I have to tell you that these days artists like you, with integrity and depth, they just aren't selling."

What?

One moment she was basking in the glow of all of his wonderful praise, and the next moment her hopes were shattered.

She went to her default position. Attitude.

"You wasted a lunch if you thought that was an easy way to let me down."

"No!" He looked horrified. "No. I do want to work with you, but the choice is not completely mine as to whether or not that can happen. You see, back in the good ol' days of country music, you could walk a song into a radio station, and if the DJs got excited about new songs and new artists, they could make the decision whether or not to play the song. They were real music lovers. But somewhere along the way, radio programmers at syndicated radio stations took over and created a homogenized sound."

"Homogenized?" She couldn't help herself—her attitude was dissolving as he talked. "Like milk?"

He laughed. "Yeah, that's one way of putting it. Bland and white, no matter what carton you open."

"Oh," she said.

"The business is run by a handful of men. I wouldn't let any daughter of mine, if I had one, within a hundred feet of most of those radio guys. They aren't all bad, but there are enough bad apples in that group to make it hard to break through if you're not willing to play ball with the alpha dogs. Besides that, radio today can be summed up in one word. *Bro-country.*"

"Bro-country? Was that why I didn't see any female artists on the music videos in the reception area?"

"You are sharp," he said. "The whole thing is completely out of balance. The list of female artists who are doing well is very short, and they all have something unique. Carrie Underwood had the massive machine of *American Idol* that catapulted her to success. Miranda Lambert has this legit redneck fire that men and women just dig— she's like a modern-day Tammy Wynette, and it's for real. Then there's Taylor Swift. She's beautiful and talented and she had her daddy's money."

Elle wondered if that was an insult directed at her, then realized it couldn't be. The Taylor Swift story was well known: her dad had made shrewd investments in a girl with huge potential. It was exactly what Elle and her father were trying to do, but with one difference. Steven Adams was trying to be low-key about backing Elle.

Tommy continued. "You need to know that when Grant asked you how you'd feel about being a blond, it was the first of many requests. Label execs make decisions not on their gut anymore but on surveys and statistical studies that determine whether fans prefer blonds or brunettes. You're a beautiful brunette. I think that's refreshing. We haven't had a big star that was a brunette since Martina. But if their surveys tell them brunette won't work, they are going to want you to be blond."

"Should you be telling me this?" Elle asked.

He grinned. "Probably not. Sometimes I feel like a round peg in a company full of square holes. But I want you to be prepared. You need to figure out how much you are willing to change to chase this beast."

Elle took a deep breath and watched a homeless man pushing a cart down the street. Tommy followed her gaze.

"We call him Johnny Cash, because he tells the tourists they can meet Johnny Cash and then he says his name is Johnny and he'd love some cash. Makes the tourists giggle, and they usually hand him something. He's been around for years. He hangs out around Music Row and the park during the day, and he naps on a bench. Then he heads downtown to the mission for dinner, and he finds a warm place to sleep at night. He seems okay with his life. With who he is."

Tommy stared intently at Elle. "So my question for you is this. Are you okay with who you are? Do you know what you really want out of music?

Are you willing to give up who you are for success in the business?"

As he said that, he pointed up Music Row to the original location of the Country Music Hall of Fame. "Fame doesn't mean much if you lose your soul in the process. I'm probably the only guy at the label that will say that to you."

Elle watched as Johnny Cash disappeared around the corner. She wondered if she knew the answers to Tommy's questions.

Eight

Elle stood beside her car and glared at the parking ticket under the wiper. As if her lunch with Tommy hadn't put her in a bad enough mood already. When her phone vibrated she almost didn't look at it. The kind of day she was having, it couldn't be good news. It vibrated again, and she fished it out of her purse.

street gig?

Elle didn't get a lot of text messages. She had met a lot of people in Nashville but hadn't really made many friends. In many ways she was still the shy girl from Minnesota, just not as chubby. Not chubby at all actually.

This text was from Jim Webb, the Canadian guy about her age whom she'd met almost on her first day in Nashville. Great musician. They hadn't gotten along very well at first, but he'd grown on her. He'd written and produced a song called "Rock the Boat," and that had landed him a deal with the same pop label she'd been on. Difference was, when that pop label had folded, she'd moved on to a new label, and he was still in the hunt.

Elle pulled the parking ticket from the windshield. She'd have to pay it so that her father wouldn't find out she'd been careless enough to let it happen.

A new text pinged.

come on. just once. try it. unleash your amazing vocals on the world. usual place. 1:30.

Street gig. That was Webb's slyly humorous way of describing the age-old tradition of busking. Sit on a corner, play some music, and wait for tourists to toss money at you.

Elle knew her father would disapprove. No daughter of Steven Adams—he often referred to himself in third person—should act like a common beggar. Not when Steven Adams could afford to invest in her music career and a run at stardom.

Well, shoot. Why not unleash her vocals? It would be fun.

Nine

The usual place was a spot on 2nd Avenue in the downtown core, across from a famous bar called Coyote Ugly.

To get there from the restaurant where she'd left her car, she walked down Demonbreun Street. Yeah, that was a name that immediately let people know if you were new to town.

Elle had first pronounced it demon-bruin, thinking maybe it was some kind of old-fashioned way of describing an evil bear.

Nope. Not demon-bruin.

De-mawn-bree-une. Four distinct syllables. With emphasis on the second syllable. De-*mawn*-bree-une.

Too bad there wasn't a singer-songwriter's guide to Nashville that had that kind of insider information. When people had giggled at her bad pronunciation, she'd felt no differently than when kids in sixth grade had teased her about her weight.

The sunshine and breeze on her face were a great cure for her irritation. She passed the Bridgestone Arena where the Nashville Predators played, and she dreamed about being a guest singer between the first and second periods. She passed the Johnny Cash Museum—the real Johnny Cash, not the homeless guy—and strolled by restaurants with outdoor patios. People crowded the sidewalks, and the smell of hot dogs wafted by from the vendors on street corners.

About a block from Coyote Ugly she heard Webb's music.

Street gig.

Elle smiled. Because she'd enjoyed the show a few other times, she knew what she'd see as she got closer. If only the tourists clustered around the two musicians knew how special it was. Much more than just a street gig.

Webb wasn't playing alone, and Elle knew why.

At the beginning of the year, Webb had found someone else playing guitar on "his" corner, a place where he'd busked before. Webb had told her that the older guy seemed homeless, maybe an alcoholic. Scruffy and long-haired, with a ballcap pulled low on his face as if he was embarrassed to have to busk for change. So Webb had given the guy coffee and a breakfast bagel, and they'd become friends before Webb knew who the guy really was.

Now, as Elle got closer, she caught a glimpse of the older guy through the crowd around them. He was wearing an old gray T-shirt, and she saw his thin, ropy arms and the ballcap low on his face. He was playing some soft background chords with Webb on lead guitar and vocals.

Elle knew those muscles were from diligent exercise, and the ballcap was low so no one would recognize him. His name was Harley Hays. A generation before, he'd been a major country star with plenty of gold records. Now Harley busked for the joy of playing. As he had explained to Elle, the street corner was different than the stage, where you could impress people with your reputation, light show, sound system and band of world-class musicians. On a street corner, you were only as good as your guitar playing and your voice.

Webb was halfway through a sad song called "Tuesday Afternoon," about spending time with a girl in a coffee shop and being forlorn with unrequited love. Common enough theme, but he'd put it together in an uncommonly haunting and mesmerizing way.

Webb must have been watching for her. When he saw her, he made eye contact and smiled without breaking rhythm.

That was when she felt a hand on her butt.

A hand that rudely cupped her on the left side.

She whirled to look into the face of a wobbling drunk guy wearing a Hooters T-shirt. Midtwenties. Face red from booze. Crooked, dirty teeth.

Her good mood instantly disappeared. Without hesitation, she whipped her right hand across his face, trying to slap off the stupid grin.

She knew the impact of her palm against his skin must have been loud, because it was audible above the music.

Webb stopped playing, and all eyes turned to her and the Hooters guy, who was rubbing his face in disbelief.

The guy opened his mouth to snarl at her. "B—"

"No," Elle snapped before he could complete the word. "Say anything that rhymes with *itch*, and the next one's a punch, not a slap."

Hooters Guy took half a step closer, and somehow Webb was instantly there.

"Might want to back away," Webb said quietly to Hooters Guy. Elle had only heard that kind of cold steel in Webb's voice once before, when her father had first met him at the Pancake Pantry, back in January.

Now, though, she didn't care whether Webb was cold steel. She was mad that men wanted her to look different so she could sell music and make them money. She was mad that her father now seemed to regard her as a business invest-ment. She was mad that being female meant she was excluded in the country music industry. She was mad that someone had grabbed her butt because she was female. And she was mad that Webb assumed she needed protection.

"And you," she said to Webb, matching him in coldness, "might want to back away yourself. I've got this handled, and I don't need your help or anyone else's."

Webb blinked and wisely said nothing.

She turned on Hooters Guy. "You have anything to say?"

"Uh," he said. Already the deep-red outline of her hand was forming on his already-red face. Any other time, it would have struck her as funny. Almost looked like a handprint had been painted across his cheek.

"Starts with a *sss* sound and rhymes with the name Laurie."

"Uh," he said again.

"Maybe," she said, "we'll continue this conversation at a police station? Unless I hear the magic word. Starts with *s*, rhymes with Laurie."

"Ssss." He let the *ssss* drag out while he struggled to understand what word Elle was referring to. "Oh. Sorry."

"Apology not accepted," she answered. "But I won't take this any farther."

Without saying goodbye to Webb or Harley, she walked away.

And hated the fact that Hooters Guy was probably staring at her butt.

Ten

"**W**hat girl doesn't like to play dress-up?" Kara Kat, the perky, redheaded stylist said to Elle.

Elle was in the boardroom at Starstruck, trying not to look terrified as she stared at the rack of clothes that Kara had brought for the meeting. Elle was holding her arms up over her head as a man named Brian, who wore eyeliner and chandelier earrings, did a thorough job of measuring her from chest to toe.

Kara was the stylist to lots of top country music stars, and Brian was her assistant. Kara had agreed—with some arm-twisting, Bernie said—to take Elle on as a client.

Kara pulled a pair of ragged Daisy Duke shorts and a see-through blouse from the rack.

She added some new but made-to-look-worn cowboy boots and a long necklace with a small heart dangling from the bottom. The price tags were staggering, but the label was paying, so Elle wasn't going to worry about it.

"Now this is our classic hot-bod look," Kara said. "It's a trend getting the most clicks in videos now. The more skin the better, honey. Stylewise, keep it simple and let your body take center stage. Women love to imagine being you, and guys love to imagine being with you."

Elle heard her mother's voice inside her head. *Show class, not trash.* Hearing her voice brought back that surge of sorrow. Her mother hadn't died that long ago. Elle didn't mind the sorrow. What she was scared of was losing the sound of her mother's voice. Then her mother would truly be gone.

Show class, not trash. Elle liked her body, but she wasn't sure she could ever feel comfortable wearing something so revealing. It seemed, well, trashy.

"Now this is our girl-next-door look." Kara pulled out a very short baby-doll dress in a small floral print and a pair of white denim shorts, also ragged at the bottom. The shorts were just long enough to be visible beneath the hem of the dress. "With these, we'd put your hair in messy braids, and you'd be barefoot. Men just love sweet women in bare feet."

Elle felt only a little better about the baby-doll dress. Why did everything have to be so short?

Finally, Kara pulled out a pair of black leather leggings, a black tank top and some slick-looking black cowboy boots. "This is our vixen look. Strong and powerful. Men love a woman who can be strong as well as soft and sexy. But let's face it, sometimes a man likes a woman he thinks could kick his butt."

Not Hooters Guy, Elle thought. He definitely hadn't liked it.

Brian nodded his head in agreement and gave an exaggerated eye roll. "Oh, yeah."

Elle gagged at the thought of wearing such a hideous outfit. Every single outfit Kara had showed her was designed to appeal to men. As if no women listened to country music.

Elle swallowed hard and gathered her courage. "Do you have anything that's a little less revealing? Like maybe some distressed jeans and a simple flowery top, maybe off the shoulder to show a little skin but not too suggestive?"

Kara looked at her as if she was an idiot. "Honey, that look has been done to death. It's outdated, old-fashioned. If that's the way you want to go, then I am probably not the right stylist for the job. They hire me because I know what gets a reaction. Let's face it, in a male-dominated market, we girls have got to use all the goodies nature gave us to get where we want to go. Right?"

Elle was trying to process what Kara had said when Bernie burst into the boardroom, carrying a stack of photographs Elle immediately recognized.

"So, Kara, how are we doing with our project?" Bernie asked, completely ignoring Elle.

Kara cleared her throat. "Well, I am doing fine. Not so sure about your client. She might be feeling a little scared about the look I am suggesting."

"Oh, don't worry about that now. I'll talk to Elle. She'll come around." Bernie put his arm around Elle with a cheesy smile and said, "Right, Elle? Everything's gonna be just fine."

Elle said nothing, and he took that as a yes.

Bernie turned back to Kara. "I brought some pictures that Elle had done a couple of months ago so that you can see how she photographs."

Kara took the pictures from Bernie and started to look through them with a less-than-impressed expression on her face. Halfway through, she reached for a pencil that had been hidden in her tousle of flaming-red hair. She made a note at the corner of one photograph, then turned to Bernie.

"Can I keep these? I'd like to show them to a couple of photographers I have in mind."

"Sure, whatever you need, doll. I'm at your service." He gave her a grin that implied more.

As Kara and Brian were putting the clothes back on hangers and into the garment bags, Elle picked up one of the photos sitting on top of Kara's bag. She was curious about what Kara might have written on it, but all she saw were two capital letters on the bottom-right corner.

LF.

Eleven

Elle had set the alarm on her cell to wake her up at 7:00 AM so she could go for a run, shower, get ready and still have time to work on a few ideas for her writing appointment.

When she had first learned about it, she could hardly believe that the label had arranged for her to write with Chad Brooks, one of Nashville's most sought-after songwriters. Then Bernie had explained that it was purely a business decision. Royalties were essentially divided into publishing rights for the song and performing rights for the artist. An artist without songwriting credits made less money, which meant the manager made less money. So no way was Bernie going to let Elle be part of an album where she didn't have songwriting credits.

Even if it meant that Elle sat in a session and only contributed three lines to a song.

From what she'd read in *Billboard* magazine and heard through the grapevine, with pop music it was all about the producer and his ability to make a song, even an average pop song, into a hit. But in Nashville the song was the most important thing, and that meant the songwriter was king.

Elle knew she had a lot to learn. She felt nervous, excited and terrified all at the same time at the thought of writing with a songwriting giant like Chad Brooks. But she also wanted to be prepared, to go in with at least three solid ideas they could work on. And the best way to come up with ideas was to clear her head by going for a run through Centennial Park. It was away from the Gulch and closer to the west end, where there were antique-book stores and famous music clubs and the best high-end thrift-store shopping in town.

As she ran through Centennial, she watched an elderly man feeding the ducks by the pond. Young mothers with toddlers in strollers talked together nearby. She thought about how desperately she wanted to make her music dream a reality. Today's songwriting session could hold the key to her future. What if they wrote the next big hit today? She could barely wait to finish her run and get back to the condo to work on her ideas.

She was still in that same bubble of hope when she arrived at the Firehouse a few hours later. The famous building no longer had anything to do with firefighters, but it was famous on Music Row. It had been the old home of the beloved Nashville Fire Department before Sony Music had renovated it for use as a song-writing hub—a place for writers to meet and compose.

She had checked in with the receptionist, a sixtysomething woman named Lila, who walked Elle to the writers' rooms.

Because the building was owned by a huge player in the music world, Elle was surprised that the rooms weren't sleek and polished like the offices at the record labels. Instead, they all had small windows, drab furniture, dingy carpets and worn-out-looking upright pianos.

It looked as if the rooms had been decorated by someone's grandmother in the 1970s and hadn't changed since. Lila took Elle to a room that had her name and Chad's marked on the outside of the door and told her if she needed anything to let her know.

Elle settled in, tuning her guitar and running through her ideas softly. Thinking about all the great songs that had been written inside these walls was intimidating. But as insecurity began to creep up on her, she battled it by telling herself she could write something just as good.

Elle checked her phone. Ten fifteen. Their appointment had been for ten. Elle remembered Bernie saying that Nashville is very relaxed. Chad was probably just fashionably late.

But when she checked her watch at ten thirty, she started to be concerned. Had she gotten the day wrong? The time wrong? That seemed unlikely, since Bernie had called her the night before to remind her to be at her appointment on time. Now she shot a text to Gretchen in Tommy's office to make sure she had the time right.

She decided to venture out into the main area where there was a pool table, maybe left over from the original firehouse.

She was standing by the pool table, looking out into the parking lot and wondering what kind of car a writer like Chad Brooks might drive, when she heard a voice behind her.

"Hey there, you waiting on someone?"

Elle turned around and saw a woman in a long hippie-style skirt and Birkenstocks. She looked to be between thirty and forty, with long blond hair in braids and kind blue eyes.

Elle extended her hand, remembering her manners. "Hello, I'm Elle. Yes, I'm waiting on someone, but I don't think he's coming."

The woman extended a hand in return. "I'm Marsha. Nice to meet you, Elle. Is this your first time writing in the Firehouse?"

"Yes. I'm kind of nervous." Elle couldn't believe she had just said that, but for some reason it had come out easily. She felt very at ease with this woman.

"Elle, would you mind my asking who you are waiting on today?"

"Chad Brooks. He and I were scheduled to write at ten."

"I know Chad. Great writer," Marsha said as she looked down at a small watch with a brown leather band. "Well, it's ten forty-five. He's quite late.

Any chance there could have been a mix-up with the day or time? Maybe eleven instead of ten?"

Elle shook her head. "No, my manager called me last night to confirm the details. It was definitely ten."

Marsha looked off into the street for a moment and then said, "I'm writing by myself today. Would you like to take a swing at writing with me? Then it wouldn't be a waste of your time today. How would you feel about that?"

Before Elle could respond, her cell vibrated with an incoming text from Gretchen at Tommy's office. **Chad can't make it today.**

Elle's bubble of hope burst. There could be a million good reasons that Chad wasn't able to make it, but it still felt like a personal rejection. And Marsha was waiting for answer.

Elle didn't know anything about this woman. She might not even be any good. She certainly didn't look like a country writer. And suddenly Elle was in a bad mood.

"I'm so sorry," she said. "I'm going to have to go. Maybe some other time?"

Marsha shook her head, like she knew Elle was giving her the brush-off, but she didn't seem offended.

Elle grabbed her guitar case and her bag, said a quick goodbye and rushed out the door. So much for her first big writing appointment.

Stood up.

The Firehouse was a fitting metaphor for a career that seemed to be going up in flames.

Twelve

"Elle, you don't look too happy," Webb said.

"I'm pretty close to wanting you to call me Charlene," she answered. "Elle McWilliam isn't having much fun as a signed artist. I remember Charlene Adams used to enjoy playing music."

The two of them were back at Centennial Park. Webb told Elle he went there a lot because it had free Wi-Fi and he couldn't afford to go over the data limit on his plan.

They were sitting on a bench that overlooked a huge pond filled with ducks that had to dodge the remote-controlled toy boats that nerdy guys were racing from one end to the other.

Opposite them was the Parthenon, a full-size replica of the temple in Athens, Greece.

Elle had thought it was weird, seeing all those stone columns, until Webb explained that Nashville prided itself on being the "Athens of the South." Over a hundred years earlier there had been replicas in Nashville of most of ancient Greece's famous buildings. Webb was full of weird info.

"Huh," Webb said, tilting his face upward to enjoy the warmth of the sun. "If Elle McWilliam isn't enjoying life, that might explain why she nearly got in a fistfight yesterday with some drunk bozo and then almost punched me when I tried to help."

"If you're asking for an apology, you won't get one." Elle grinned. "Okay, a small one. I'm sorry. A little. But if I tried to explain, you wouldn't understand."

Webb opened his eyes. He was a good-looking guy, but Elle wasn't interested in him except as a friend. She knew Webb liked a girl he'd met in Alabama, some long-distance thing he didn't talk about.

"Try me," Webb said.

"When was the last time you worried that an extra inch on your waist would change how the world treats you?"

"Aah," he said.

"It's all about bro-country these days," she said. "Drives me crazy."

"Aah," he said again.

"Does it bother you that you don't have a deal anymore?" she asked.

"Not so much," Webb said. "Sounds clichéd, but I'm just enjoying each day of the journey instead of wondering where the road is going to take me. I've got a sweet situation that allows me to live on a houseboat rent-free. I've got some good friends in town. I've also got some songs already produced that I can sell if I want to, and I'm working to finish my album. If something comes along, great. If not, I'm okay. For me, it's all about the music anyway. I'll worry about getting a mortgage and a career later. For now, I just want to make music for the sake of making music."

Elle sighed, wishing she could feel such freedom. "I hear you," she said. She told him about the missed appointment with Chad Brooks and about the woman who had offered to write with her.

"Hang on," Webb said. "Marsha? Marsha Chapman?"

"Didn't catch her last name," Elle said. "Blond braids. Looked to be about midthirties."

Webb picked up his phone, typed for a minute and then held the phone up to Elle. "That her?"

"Yeah."

"Okay, for starters, she's midforties, but I could have a serious crush on her," Webb said. "Second, any idea how many hits she's written? I'd kill to have a songwriting session with her."

Elle groaned. "Seriously? I turned her down."

Webb was thoughtful and silent for a few moments. Then he said, "Don't take a swing at me when I ask you my question, okay? But it's an important question, so I'll take the chance."

"Sure," Elle said.

"Any chance you turned her down because you bought into the bro-country crap and assumed because she wasn't a guy she wasn't any good?"

Thirteen

There was a quote Elle remembered from a book she'd read in high school. *If you don't know where you're going, any road will get you there.*

Elle felt a bit like she was living out those words as she slid down in the chair at the salon. Lydia, one of Nashville's top colorists, showed Elle a swatch guide for shades of blond.

Elle wasn't exactly sure what she wanted or where she was headed. She had been telling herself all morning that maybe this road was as good as any, that she should see where it might lead. Elle fought frustration. Bernie had sent over a girl from his office to make sure Elle didn't bolt out the door before they had a chance to apply the peroxide. Maybe that's why Bernie was the best, Elle thought—he anticipated problems.

Elle tried not to imagine the amount of damage involved in turning her very dark hair into the golden-blond shade they were recommending.

The hairdresser's own hair was kind of alarming and didn't fill Elle with confidence. Cut in a short bob, it was dyed red on one side and platinum blond on the other. If that was the way things were going, Elle was in trouble.

As Lydia mixed up the chemicals and pulled on rubber gloves, she said to Elle, "It's a tough business out there these days. I don't envy you trying to fight your way into the boys' club."

The stylist at the next chair nodded her head in agreement. She was snipping the hair of a fashionable older woman who looked to be the proud recipient of some very good plastic surgery.

Lydia went on. "I mean, these days it's a dog-eat-dog world on Music Row. Those good ol' boys have taken over the entire country-music industry. They go out in their camo gear for days at a time, camping out, hunting for deer, wiping deer blood on their faces like some sort of war paint. Drinking beer and writing their hits around the campfire at night. No women allowed. Soooo redneck."

Elle blurted out something that had been bothering her. "Is Chad Brooks a good-ol'-boy kind of writer? Does he ever write with female songwriters?"

"Him?" Lydia said. "Well, he can do whatever he likes, as many hits as he's had. I think he does sometimes write with a female artist if he thinks it's worth his time and he thinks the label is on board."

The older woman in the chair spoke up. Her accent was strong like that of the genteel ladies from the Deep South who wore pearls and red lipstick and sounded like old movie stars. "My husband sometimes golfs with Chad. They belong to the same country club, you see. Just yesterday Chad was telling my husband that he had been booked to write with some new young artist, a gal he'd never heard of. But then he heard her label was in trouble, and he decided not to bother. So he went golfing with my husband instead." She laughed, as if it was the most delightful story.

"Yesterday morning?" Lydia said. "Won't take long for word about that label to spread through town."

Yesterday morning, Elle thought, Chad dumped me to go golfing. Her next thought was, The label is in trouble?

She considered getting out of the chair, but it was too late. Lydia had just added the last few chemicals to Elle's cherished brunette hair.

Fourteen

lle held a cup of chai tea as she sat and watched the rain stream down her condo window. No run this morning for her. The rain seemed a fitting backdrop for her mood. Her label was going under? When was Bernie going to tell her? To top it off, she could barely stand to look in the mirror. The blond staring back at her looked pretty good, but it wasn't her. Lydia had told Elle she should get a spray tan. Pale skin, which had looked fine with her dark hair, would look a bit washed out now that she was a blond.

Everything was unraveling. She looked at her guitar in the corner. She didn't even want to play. As she stared out the window, her phone buzzed behind her. She didn't recognize the number, but it was a Nashville area code, so she picked up.

"Hello?"

"Hi, is this Elle? This is Marsha Chapman. We met the other day at the Firehouse."

Elle stood up, remembering the conversation she'd had with Webb about Marsha.

"Marsha. I'm so glad you called."

"I hope you don't mind, but Tommy, your A&R guy, gave me your number. I'm calling because he sent over a few of your songs, and I have to tell you, I was really impressed. Your voice and your songs have a very genuine and unique quality to them. I wondered if you would like to take a swing at writing together sometime?"

"I'm so sorry about the other day," Elle said. "I was embarrassed about being stood up by Chad Brooks, and I think I was rude to you."

"You were polite even when you were rude," Marsha said with a laugh.

"Also, I heard something yesterday that might change your mind about working with me. My label is folding, so I might not have a contract."

"Aah. That is bad news."

"I don't want you to feel like you're wasting your time with me."

"Elle, I've been doing this a while, and what I believe more than anything is that great songs and great artists find their way to an audience. I don't care whether you have a deal or not. Tommy really believes in you. You're genuinely talented. That's what it's about for me."

Elle took a moment to absorb those words before she spoke. "Thanks, Marsha. But how can I make a career for myself without a label? I can't see the point of writing if there's no record to write for."

Marsha said, "How you move forward depends on one thing. I apologize if this offends you, but I have to ask. Do you want to be a great artist or a star?"

Elle turned the question over in her mind. She thought about Webb and how much joy he had when he made music.

Marsha continued. "You open to giving that some thought? I'd be happy to talk about it when we get together."

Outside, the thunder boomed against the window as she sat in silence, unable to answer Marsha's question. How long would it take her to figure it out?

Fifteen

Hey, cowboy, hang your hat on my heart and throw your boots under my bed...

Facing a cameraman, Elle sang along to the loud blare of the boom box behind the cameras. The boom box seemed old school, but that's how it was done.

She moved from a stove to the kitchen sink, holding a black cast-iron skillet in pink oven mitts. The point of singing along was to ensure that the lip syncing was accurate when the music was dubbed into the video. "This love we've got has me in over my head..."

Without warning, the music stopped.

"I'm not seeing a smile," the director, a guy named Derek Lake, said. "You have to sell the giddiness of your love. Nothing makes you happier than cooking your man a meal. Got it?"

Lake was a short man, maybe in his forties, with hair gooped into a swirl like an Elvis wannabe. He wore a long-sleeved polo shirt with the cuffs folded up, blue jeans and ostrich-leather cowboy boots. He had a habit of slapping the palm of his right hand against his thigh as he spoke.

"Giddiness," Elle said. At the prospect of cooking a man a meal? Yeah right.

"And we need some swish," Lake said. "A smile that shows giddiness and some swishiness in the hips. We've got three cameras going. Your body has to scream desire."

"Desire." So much desire it made her want to cook? Yeah right.

The kitchen was a set. The cameramen were standing behind tripods. A makeup girl was at a table behind them. Bernie was next to her, leaning over to whisper something in her ear. Kara Kat and her assistant Brian hovered back there too. With such a big crowd watching, desire was the last thing on Elle's mind. Self-consciousness, on the other hand, was near the top of the list.

Elle wanted to tug at her shorts. It felt like they were riding up and half her butt cheeks were exposed. This wasn't a music video—it was more like a commercial for Hooters.

"Giddiness and swish," Elle repeated. "Got it." She tried to keep the scorn out of her voice, but some of it must have leaked out.

"Hang on!" Bernie said. He'd turned up just after the shoot started, telling Lake he was there in an official capacity. Elle thought he just wanted to check out her rear end in the tight shorts.

"Lakers," Bernie said, "give me a minute with her."

Lakers. What was it about grown men and the stupid nicknames they gave each other? Not much creativity to the nicknames either. Most ended in -*ers*, or -*sie*. Maybe someone needed to come up with an app to convert guys' last names into nicknames. Webb would be Webbsie. Maybe she'd start calling him that.

Bernie crooked his finger at Elle, so she turned to Derek Lake instead. When was Bernie going to learn she wasn't his puppet?

"Sure, Lakers," she said. "I've got it. Giddiness and swish."

She enjoyed the slight frown on Lake's face when she used his nickname. It was like a secret handshake. You couldn't use it unless you were part of the club. The boys' club.

"We need a break anyway," Lake said. He slapped his palm against his thigh for emphasis and stepped aside, leaving her alone under the lights in the fake kitchen.

Elle went to the stove to set down the cast-iron skillet, aware that Bernie was staring at her butt.

When she turned, he was right there.

"Look," he said. "Normally, I'm a patient guy. Normally, I can put up with attitude."

"Attitude?"

"You heard me," he said. "Attitude. You do realize that the label isn't behind us anymore, right? Let me repeat. This is not a label shoot. It's an investment by your father. That means he is paying big bucks for a top-rate video to make sure you get signed someplace else. But I'm almost to the point where I don't care how much your father is willing to shell out, because I don't know any label that's going to want to work with you. If you're going to be a diva, you have to earn it first. Understand? If you walk away from me this time, I'm not going to chase you down."

"Diva? I'm a diva because I don't want my music video to be soft porn for rednecks?"

Bernie exploded. "That's exactly what I'm talking about! You realize how many other singers would give one of their kidneys for an opportunity like this?"

Elle noticed that a couple of the cameramen had swung their heads to catch the argument.

"Good trade. A kidney for a chance to show my cleavage and parade around a kitchen. Tell me why these shorts are called Daisy Dukes."

Her question seemed to throw Bernie slightly off balance. "What? Because Daisy Duke made them famous."

"In a television show called *The Dukes of Hazzard*, right?"

"Right."

"That would be the same show with a car with a Confederate flag across the hood," Elle said. "Shouldn't that tell you something about Daisy Dukes and a racist redneck South that I don't want to represent?"

Bernie inhaled deeply, visibly trying to control himself. "You don't even have the faintest clue what we're trying to do here, do you?"

"I have a pretty good idea."

"No." He spat out the word. "You don't. A few days ago, you had to ask me what it meant when someone wrote *LF* on a photo. You'll notice I didn't answer."

"Then go ahead and tell me," Elle said.

"You're a girl with a great voice and the chance to make it big if you can project the right image. I gave Lakes specific instructions to do everything possible to put you in a good light. It's not like you're Miss America here. The lighting, the camera angles. Everything is designed to hide what you're going to have to fight your whole career. And I'm only telling you what *LF* means because I'm good and mad and about to quit, no matter what your father pays me. And trust me, if I can't get you a label deal, no one can."

"Tell me," Elle said. "What does *LF* mean?"

"Two words," he answered. She was aware that the video crew was listening as he continued to speak. "*Looks fat.*"

*　*　*

Elle dropped the two-hundred-dollar pair of Daisy Dukes in the trash. She needed a hot shower to wash away the three pounds of makeup and tanning lotion and hair products she had endured to become a perfect dream woman for rednecks to drool over.

Back at the studio, with Bernie's insult ringing in her ears, she had done at least thirty takes of "Hang Your Hat on My Heart," feeling like a raving bimbo the whole time. When she'd decided they had enough footage for the video—or, at least, all that she ever planned to give them—she had stormed out of the video shoot, leaving Lake, Bernie and everyone else in shock. She had fought the urge to flip them all off as she left. What Bernie had told her had really hurt, especially since he'd done it in front of everyone at the studio. It was like being back in middle school again.

Bernie had no idea what it was like to eat the same things all your skinny friends ate and then have to run three extra miles to keep the weight off when your friends stayed thin.

Now the water ran over her body and she looked down at herself. Her waist was small, and her hips were what her mother had called "womanly." She missed her mom. All this would have been a lot easier with her mother at her side.

Looks. Fat.

Two words that could inflict so much pain. *Looks. Fat.*

Easy to stand off to the side and treat a person like a two-dimensional object. Like a product. Something to market, to perfect. Well, she wasn't going to be their little science experiment anymore. She knew what she had to do.

She jumped out of the shower, dried off and stood in her towel, too impatient even to dress as she searched for the phone number she wanted in her cell. It rang a few times and then she said, "Marsha...this is Elle. I think I have an answer for you. I would love to write a song with you, and I finally know exactly what I want to say."

Sixteen

Elle had a melody in her head and she'd written a few words to prepare for her appointment with Marsha.

Marsha had booked a nice room at the Firehouse with a few windows, to let in some much-needed sunshine, and an old upright piano in the corner. Marsha sat at the piano as Elle told her what had been going on—the video shoot, the label, Bernie. How they'd tried to fit her into a mold that felt like a coffin. Nothing she said seemed to surprise Marsha.

"I am so sorry this is happening to you, Elle," Marsha said. "I've heard this story many times before, but it often happens to artists who really don't have any sort of true talent. That's what doesn't make sense about your situation.

I know Tommy sees your talent. Honestly, I think everyone else has decided to drink the Kool-Aid."

Elle looked up from her guitar. "Pretty much."

"The question is whether you're going to drink it along with them."

"How about no."

"I knew there was a reason I liked you," Marsha said. "So what are you working on? You said you might have an idea or two."

"Well, I have part of the verse music and a few ideas for lyrics."

Elle played and sang a few phrases that she thought sounded good but didn't necessarily all go together.

"Sing me the chorus again," Marsha said. "The rest of it isn't quite there yet."

Elle did as requested.

"I like that, Elle. But..."

"The dreaded *but*." Elle laughed. "I'm okay with it. I get little phrases that feel right and are what I want to say, but it feels like a puzzle. I'm not quite sure what the other pieces are."

Marsha nodded. "There are a lot of different ways to approach writing a song. And what you just said—that's totally normal. Writing for a competitive market is very difficult. Lots of people have been doing it for twenty or thirty years. But there are a few key steps that can make the process go a lot smoother and feel less intimidating."

"I'm sure listening."

"The phrases you were singing are a great beginning. They sound like they're going somewhere. The hardest part about writing a song is knowing what it's about. What's this one about for you?"

"It's about something that my mom always told me," Elle said. "She died when I was was in high school. I've been thinking about her a lot lately. Wishing she were here. She always used to tell me that I had to be true to myself. I want to write about that. It seems like I've been losing myself since I got to Nashville."

Marsha nodded her head again and reached out to pat Elle's knee. "Let's write something that would make your momma proud."

A writing session was almost like a therapy session, Elle thought, and for some reason she was totally comfortable sharing personal things with Marsha.

"I think that's an important message for a lot of people—staying true to yourself," Marsha said. "Nobody gets tired of that theme. The trick is to say it in a new way. As for getting those feelings into a song format, maybe tackling the chorus first will make the verses easier to write."

"I never thought of that."

"The chorus expresses the revelation of the song. But..."

"But?"

"Even before you begin to write the chorus, there is one very important element you need to decide on," Marsha said. "Songwriting 101. You need a hook. In all music, but especially in country music, it's all about the hook. The hook is the core idea—usually a twist on a familiar phrase that expresses the heart of your song."

"Like 'Hey, cowboy, hang your hat on my heart and throw your boots under my bed.'"

"That's a hook that makes me cringe," Marsha said. "More for what it expresses than anything else. But yes, in the market that likes those kind of songs, it's an effective hook."

"Except I don't want to write songs for that market."

"Same principle though. We need to figure out a phrase that drives toward the verses and the chorus. The hook usually comes at the very end of the chorus in country music. Pop music often starts with a hook that shows up in the chorus. Since we're writing for the country music market, let's save that hook for the end."

Songwriting 101. Elle was more than okay with that.

"Now tell me again what your mother used to tell you." Marsha said.

Elle answered, "To be true to myself."

"Hmm. It would be nice if we had an internal rhyme in the hook. Something that rhymed with *true*."

"*Blue*?"

"I like that. But..."

Elle laughed. "But?"

"But if we are using that phrase, then we have to find clever ways to mention color in a way that makes the hook seem fresh. Now play the chorus again, if you don't mind."

Marsha tinkered on the piano as Elle continued to play the melody on the guitar. When Marsha stopped, Elle took the hint and stopped too.

Marsha said, "Let's go with the phrase 'You say' again. We'll make the phrase part of the chorus as another small melodic and lyrical hook. And because we're repeating the first two words of the phrase and melody several times, it will be easier for people to remember."

Marsha played the melody at the piano and sang:

You say you don't want me
You say you don't love me
You say that I don't fit the picture you've got

"I can hear it," Elle said when she stopped singing. "I'm just waiting for you to say *but.*"

Marsha grinned. "Not at all. Now we need another set of lines that are like the first three. The only word we have to rhyme is the last word of the third line. Our rhyme will be *got*, but it would be great if we wrote lines that use the same phrases at the beginning of lines four and five, like we did for the first lines above. So instead of *you say*, find two other memorable words for a new phrase."

Elle played the music and melody, and suddenly the words came to her and she sang:

I draw outside the lines
I draw strength from inside
And I won't become something I'm not.

Marsha gave Elle a high five. "That's amazing, Elle. You've used the analogy of art to express the deeper meaning of being an individual, and you've added an additional internal rhyme. We're getting closer. We just need to change up the music for the second half of the chorus to set up the hook."

Elle hummed the melody, and when more words came, she knew she had it. She sang for Marsha like she was Charlene again, singing alone in her room, happy to have her music.

Let me paint the picture for you
Do what you wanna do
But I'm gonna be
True blue.

* * *

The next night Elle sat outside on a bench in Centennial Park with her guitar, playing the song she and Marsha had written earlier. Over and over. The words burned in her heart and rang true. The notes floated effortlessly across her lips. Her face without makeup. Her hair in a ponytail. Without a care in the world about her image. The only thing that mattered to Elle was this song. If there was ever a song that Elle felt connected to, it was this one.

If you say you don't want me
Say you don't love me,
Say that I just don't measure up for you
ohh ohh
Well I know who I am
And I know what I'm not
Nobody's perfect like you might have thought
oohh

No matter what you say
No matter what you want
I can't let you turn me into something that I'm not
The only thing I've got for you
It's way long overdue
I won't be who I'm not
The color in my paint box

True blue
I'm gonna be true blue.

When Elle looked up from her guitar, Johnny Cash from Demonbreun Street was standing on the path across from her, a smile beaming from his face, nodding to the music.

She smiled.

Elle was finally certain what her next move should be, and there was nothing that could sway her.

Seventeen

The grilled coconut-shrimp platter was what Elle really wanted, but the waiter delivered what she had ordered instead—a single fish taco with a side salad, no dressing. That's what a person did when someone else wrote *LF* across one of her photos.

She watched with envy as the waiter gave Webb a hamburger that took two hands to hold. Webb bit into it, leaving a streak of sauce on his face.

"You attacked that like it had insulted your mother," Elle said.

"How many steps along the dock from here to my houseboat?" Webb answered. He often said strange things. Elle was getting used to the fact that Webb had a different take on life. It was best just to go along for the ride.

When people asked Webb where he lived, he liked to tell them mile marker 175 on the Cumberland River. Not many people knew that downstream from downtown Nashville was the Rock Harbor Marina, filled with houseboats. Webb was houseboat-sitting for a friend, and this was Elle's first visit to the marina.

Elle liked the vibe. It wasn't an upscale marina filled with expensive boats and snooty people in fancy clothing. Instead, it looked like a place where people enjoyed the water for the sake of enjoying the water.

The Blue Moon Waterfront Grille had that same down-to-earth vibe. She enjoyed the lack of pretension—and the big umbrella that was shielding her from the late-afternoon sun.

"How many steps?" she said. "Twenty-five? Thirty?"

"Forty-two. I eat mac and cheese just about every day, and not once do I add ketchup to my bowl without thinking that this restaurant is only forty-two steps away, serving a burger like this."

Webb studied her face.

"I don't think you're following my drift here," he said. "Mac and cheese. It's what poverty-stricken musicians eat. Every day. Because, well, they are poverty-stricken. A burger like this is a big treat for me."

She smiled. "I guess I should have parked my Beamer in a less conspicuous spot."

Webb shrugged. "One of the things I like about you and your money is that you don't think it makes you better than anyone else. But if you've never had mac and cheese, today is not the day to try it. We're celebrating."

"We?"

"Yeah," he said. "We. Looks like you and I are back together on the same label."

"Again," she said. "Still not catching your drift."

"I just got signed by your A&R guy, Tommy," Webb said. "A nice deal. Correction. A very nice deal."

Elle looked away from her fish taco and salad. She wasn't sure how to tell Webb that the label was in trouble. Would he be insulted if she offered to pick up the lunch bill? Or would it make her news easier to swallow?

"I'm so sorry, Webb," Elle finally said, "The only good thing about it is that I've lost my manager too."

"That's old news," Webb said, wiping his fingers on a napkin. "Today's news is that the label is back in business again. Some kind of corporate bailout."

"Seriously?" Elle said. "That's great for—"

Her cell buzzed. She glanced at the number. "My manager. I mean, my ex-manager. Want me to let it go through to voice mail?"

"No worries," Webb said. "Take it, and if you want to talk about anything private, go for a walk. I'll be here when you get back. Might even eat that taco if you don't want it."

"Nothing's private with Bernie," she said as she answered her phone.

"Hey," Bernie said. "Wanted to let you know we're back in business. You and me."

"You quit," Elle said. "Remember?"

"I walked," Bernie said. "Big difference. A person has to know when to cut his losses. But in case you haven't heard, the label is back, so I'm back."

"What about me?" Elle said. "What if I don't want you back?"

Across the table, Webb raised an eyebrow.

"You don't have a choice," Bernie said with a laugh. "I guess you don't read contracts that closely. Maybe your daddy's the one who reads the fine print. You're with the label, and as long as you're with the label, you're with me."

"Are we going to pretend what happened at the video shoot didn't happen? You know, those two initials on the photo."

"Oh," Bernie said. Awkward silence. "Actually, *LF* means, um, *looks fabulous*."

Elle knew the slimeball was lying and decided to give him silence instead of a response.

"That's right," Bernie said, adding energy to his voice. "Looks fabulous."

"I'll put in a call and ask," Elle said. "Just to confirm."

She wanted him to wriggle like a worm on a hook.

"Look," he said. "Even if *LF* really meant *looks fat*, you'd have no choice but to get over it. Taking stuff personally in this business will drive you crazy. But I've got to apologize. I was in a bad mood. So have a good laugh about it, and move on. We've got great things in front of us."

He hung up.

Yup. He'd lied. It did not mean *looks fabulous.* Elle stared at the phone as if it were a bottle that held a genie. An evil genie.

"That was a strange half a conversation to overhear," Webb said. "Want to talk about it?"

No, she didn't.

Elle handed Webb a clean napkin. "You have sauce on your face. It's driving me crazy."

Eighteen

"**C**an we try that verse one more time, but maybe this time leave a bit more space for the vocal to shine?" Marsha held down a red square button labeled *Talkback* so she could communicate with the musician in the booth.

Marsha had invited Elle to the production session of the demo of the song they had co-written. She wanted Elle to see it from the other side of the booth, promising Elle it would give her a better sense of the production process.

Marsha waited for a response from the guitar player, but he said nothing. Beside Marsha at the console was a bearded guy named Ronnie, the sound engineer. Ronnie seemed a sweet and gentle guy, and it made sense to Elle that he was a good friend of Marsha's.

Marsha took her hand off the red button and spoke to Elle. "He's not getting it. This is the kind of song that only needs a simple demo, and when you go simple it's important to get each part just right."

Marsha pushed down the red button again.

"Jack?" Marsha said. "You okay with leaving some space?"

The guitar player, Jack Miles, was one of Nashville's hottest new guitar players. He was young and had a tremendous amount of raw talent, but not a lot of studio experience. Marsha had explained to Elle that it took time to learn the art of playing a part that is present but not overbearing. She'd told Elle the main focus of any song needed to be the vocal.

Jack played his guitar part again. When he finished, he looked through the glass at Marsha.

Marsha hit the red button. "Okay, Jack, your tone is unbelievable. I love the lick you did, but I think we need to save that for the turnaround. Keep it simpler in the verse."

Jack played again but without any change.

Marsha hit *Talkback* again and said, "Hey, Jack, why don't you come on in here for a minute?"

Jack came out of the booth and looked over at Elle with a *Hey, babe, how you doing?* smile. He slowly ran a hand through hair that looked to have taken more time to do than Elle's.

"You must be Elle," he said. "I'm Jack Miles. I like your voice. Nice to have that kind of vocal supporting my licks."

This wasn't Elle's show. She kept her mouth shut.

Marsha spun her chair around from the console. "Okay, Jack, I am not sure if we are understanding each other. Does what I'm saying about playing simpler on the verse make sense to you?"

Jack shrugged. "I like what I'm playing. I think it's good the way I played it. Otherwise I wouldn't have played it that way three times."

Marsha took a deep breath and stood. "I understand that you know guitar, Jack. But I am the producer of this session."

Jack rolled his eyes. "Didn't know women could produce. As far as I know, there aren't any in the music business. Not anyone who is any good."

Marsha reacted with a shake of her head and an *Oh, you poor idiot* smile.

Elle pulled out her iPhone and called up Siri. "Google search. Marsha Chapman. Country music. Number-one hits."

She looked at her screen. "Hmmm. Jack, you might want to check this out. You can read, right?"

Elle handed the phone to Jack and watched his face as he absorbed the information.

"Seriously?" Jack looked back at Marsha. "Your stuff?"

"I'm not really sure what gender has to do with making music," Marsha told him. "It's about heart. I've got your address, and you'll get paid, but you won't be required anymore."

"What?" Jack looked stunned.

"I hope you learn sooner rather than later that in this town, no matter how good your guitar playing, first and foremost it's about relationships."

Jack shuffled away, and Elle realized she'd learned something important. Not only about relationships, but about how to be tough without being a jerk.

Show class, not trash, as her mother had said.

Nineteen

Elle and Tommy sat in the Starstruck conference room with the shades drawn.

Tommy smiled. "I've already seen this, so I'm excited about how much you're going to like it."

When the video started to play, Elle was shocked to see how good she looked, how good the video was. The shots of her with the good-looking guy on the porch swing, with Elle in a simple cotton dress, weren't too bad at all. She hadn't taken into account all the scenes they'd filmed outside the kitchen. Maybe she could live with it after all.

Suddenly Elle's resolve to stand behind her art felt a bit weak. The video looked just like all the stuff she saw on CMT. She would never be a fan of the Daisy Duke shorts, but she was a little surprised at how good she looked in them.

As the last notes of the song rang out, Elle said, "Wow. That looks better than I expected. Much better."

After working with Marsha, she'd felt so certain she wanted to be a real musician, an artist, not a commodity. But this video put her in a good light. Should she really turn her back on everything the label was offering?

"Here's the deal," Tommy began, jolting Elle out of her thoughts. "They want to lead with this single. The men and women in the market— Betsy in Oklahoma and Bubba in Kentucky— will all love this. They've already done some test marketing and got a big thumbs-up. I know you had reservations about this, Elle, but the execs are pumped about this video. It isn't ideal, I know. It isn't artistic, but it could get your foot in the door. Get you on people's radar, make it possible for you to pursue your artistic vision later on."

Maybe Tommy was right, Elle thought. Maybe this was the way to reach her ultimate goal. Maybe this way would be the easiest for everyone. Including herself.

Maybe she shouldn't have thrown those two-hundred-dollar Daisy Dukes in the trash after all.

"There's one small thing we need to discuss," Tommy said. "And this is going to be hard for me to tell you and hard for you to hear. And let me assure you, you're not the only artist this has ever happened to."

Elle looked at him, puzzled. "What are you trying to tell me?"

Tommy raked his hands through his hair and looked her in the eye. His own eyes looked weary and sad, as if he hadn't slept well in days. "What I'm trying to tell you, Elle, is..."

He hesitated.

"What? Just tell me."

"Elle, don't take the this wrong way. But in some of the parts of the video, they used a body double."

* * *

"I know it's the middle of the day, Dad," Elle said. "I wouldn't break your rule unless it was important, I promise."

She held the cell phone to her ear with her left hand as she picked apart the salad in front of her. The restaurant was upscale, and conversations around her were muted. No loud laughter like at the Blue Moon Waterfront Grille.

She found a strawberry. Wonderful. Eating alone at a restaurant was bad enough. But the reason for the salad was definitely the most horrible thing about the situation.

Looks fat. Not looks fabulous. Looks fat. Tommy had confirmed what it really meant.

"Five minutes," Steven Adams said on the other end of the phone. "I'm in New York, working with my stockbrokers. A quarter percent commission on the deal I'm working is going to be huge."

"Five minutes," Elle said.

"I can hear your tone," her father answered. "Don't think this makes me a bad dad. End of the day, you get all the time you need. Middle of the day, not so easy. Middle of the day, we're equals. Business partners. You know that. I'm treating you no differently than anyone else I work with. Take that as a compliment."

"Of course," she said, pushing the strawberry aside for later.

"So why are you calling?"

Because I'm lonely and confused, Elle wanted to say. *Because sometimes in the middle of the day, I need my dad.*

Instead, she answered like a business partner. "I want out of my deal with the label. How do we make it happen?"

"We don't," he said. "Anything else?"

"Don't you want to ask me some questions about why I want out of the deal?"

"Bernie and I talk every day," her dad said. "He's made it pretty clear that you are more focused on what he calls 'artistic integrity'—I'm using air quotes here—than on actually making it in the business. How much clearer do he and I have to be? Artistic integrity is a luxury you can pursue when you've established your career. Even then, it might not work. Heard of a guy named Garth Brooks?"

"Yes, but—"

"He was at the height of his career. Decided to produce a pop album. A pop album! World's most famous country singer. Millions of fans. Look it up. Gave his alter ego a name. Chris Gaines. Let's just say it didn't work for him and leave it at that. I repeat. You are in the music business. Key word—*business.*"

"What if my key word is *music*?"

"Not possible," her dad said. "Look, I've got about a minute left here before I need to go back into my meeting."

"Then tell me in ten words or less why it's not possible."

"How about four words. Ready? I own the label."

"What?"

"I bailed it out. I own a majority share. It was what was best for your career. I believe that you can sell enough music to make it worth my while to own the majority share of your record label."

Elle took a deep breath.

Her father took that opportunity to continue. "You can thank me tonight when we talk again. Really, I have to go."

"No," Elle said. "Not yet. This saves me a call to the label. I'm telling you that I want out of my contract. And you can make it happen."

"Well," he said, "I did see this coming. In a sense, I'm proud of you. Stubborn and determined to do it your way. That's how I got to where I am. But I also got here by knowing when to be stubborn and determined and when to put logic

ahead of emotion. Until you learn that, sometimes a dad needs to step in and stop a disaster
from happening. That's why I made sure that
your little friend Webb got his own offer from the
label. Because you have a simple choice. If you
walk from the deal, his deal dies too."

"You can't be serious."

"That's a business move, and it's a good one
for you. Choose wisely. I just ran out of time. Talk
later."

He hung up, leaving Elle to stare at the lonely
strawberry on the side of her plate.

Twenty

That night Elle sat in bed with her iPad in her lap, watching YouTube videos of a few artists she followed. She was feeling overwhelmed and desperately needed to process all that had happened in the last few days. She needed to find a quiet place in her mind. She was wearing black cotton pajamas that had been a gift from her mother on Elle's sixteenth birthday. Her mom had always given her new PJs on her birthday, and this was the last pair Elle had received. She missed her mom more than ever before.

She closed the iPad, picked up her guitar and began strumming the song she had written with Marsha. What would her mother say if she were here?

Elle knew the answer. She would say, *Be true to yourself, Charlene.*

Be true. Charlene.

How long had it been since someone called her by her real name, her grandmother's name? Over the last few weeks she had been everything but true to herself.

Then suddenly, like a spark to kindling, an idea ignited. It might be a terrible idea. Or it might be a brilliant idea, but whichever it was, Elle felt a surge of determination. She would send a clear message to her father and to everyone at her label.

She positioned her iPhone atop her dresser and pushed *Record.*

She returned to her bed and sat with her guitar in her arms, looking directly at the iPhone, and began to speak.

"My name is Elle. Actually, my name is Charlene, but my label here in Nashville changed it to Elle. Charlene sounded too much like someone from Minnesota, which I am.

"My hair is brunette. Yeah, I know it looks blond. The label did that too. They said my being blond would sell more records. You know what else they did? They used a body double in my video, because apparently, you are a loser if you are bigger than a size 2.

"But I shouldn't care. Because I am just a commodity to the label. Not a person. Commodities don't have feelings, right? And apparently, I'm not a valuable commodity compared to the country bros. Oh yeah. I don't drink beer, hunt deer or drive a pickup truck. And to all of you who do drink beer, hunt deer and drive pickup trucks, it's probably a great world for you. But if you also think that a woman is just an accessory to drinking beer, hunting deer and driving a pickup truck, then you're in for a big surprise. Lots of women, myself included, have no interest in your fantasies.

"My real name is Charlene and my hair is brown and my body isn't perfect, but I'm okay with that. I'm not going to go along with this charade anymore and be someone I'm not.

"And one more thing. This is for Bernie, my manager. My ex-manager. You're not fooling anybody with that comb-over. If you or anyone else tries to force me to stay with the label, I'm going to want to see everyone in Daisy Dukes at the next meeting with your label buddies. That's a promise, so if you want me to be your artist, go ahead and shave your legs."

Elle grinned at the iPhone. "And now I'm going to play a song that matters to me, a song about being true to yourself."

As Elle played the notes, her voice soared. At the end of the song she stood up, went to the dresser and pressed *Stop*.

Then she did a quick edit, took a deep breath and uploaded the video to YouTube.

There was no turning back now.

Twenty-One

The afternoon was gray, and a steady rain fell. There was no wind, and it was hot. Elle had just joined Tommy and Webb on the flat roof of Webb's houseboat, where they had a view of the harbor and the river beyond. A canopy shielded them from the rain. A perfect type of rain. Soothing.

But Elle was in a funk. Sunshine and blue sky might have helped.

She settled into a lounge chair. Webb had cut up some watermelon. She helped herself to a big chunk from the plate. It was natural sugar in the juices, she told herself. No harm in that.

"What's up with two of my favorite guys?" she asked. "You called. And now I'm here."

"We're hanging," Webb answered. "Chilling. Talking about a certain YouTube video. Telling them to shave their legs was funny. We've decided it can start a whole new genre. We've given it a name. Rant music."

"Oh," Elle said.

"Oh is right," Tommy said. "Hence the phone call. Figured it would be a lot more relaxed to talk about it here than at the label. Got to say, you really cut loose with that one. In fact, I'm taking a little heat about it. My first call was supposed to be to Bernie, but I'd rather hear from you what's behind it."

"Like Webb said, just a rant."

"Might have been better to have that rant with me over lunch or something," Tommy said. "The video is getting some serious hits. Enough that the execs heard about it. To them, it's like a stick in the eye. You're an artist on the label, and you come out against them even before your first record is released?"

"No one has anything to say about the song?"

"I did. Told them it was a great song. Something we should cut. Their reaction was simple. I think if they'd had knives, they would have stabbed me. They don't care about how you look or sound in the video. They care about how it makes them look. They want to drop you. They—"

Tommy's cell phone rang. He held the display out for Elle to read. "Bernie," Tommy said. "Think I should answer?"

"You in the mood to listen to someone lie through his teeth and tell you I didn't mean a word of it?" Elle asked. "All he wants is a deal and his commission."

"Good point." Tommy set the cell phone down and muted its ring.

Then he changed his mind and answered.

"Bernie?"

Silence as Tommy listened.

"Yeah, Bernie," Tommy said. "On one condition. You going to wear Daisy Dukes to our next meeting?"

More silence.

"Huh," Tommy said. "He hung up."

"Probably didn't want to shave his legs," Webb said.

Tommy smiled at Elle. "I can take it, then, that you meant every word of that rant?"

"Each one. Underlined."

"Man," Tommy said, "that puts me in a bad position."

"I'll make it clear you had nothing to do with it," Elle said.

"Hey," Tommy said, "I liked the song. I liked the video. I liked what you had to say. Telling off the execs probably wasn't the most politically smart thing to do, but there's stuff I'm tired of too. That's not the bad position I'm talking about. It's how what you're doing affects Webb. Which is why he and I thought it would be best if the three of us got together."

"What's weird," Webb said, "is that Tommy was told that if he didn't talk you off the ledge, my deal was gone too. He's supposed to talk you into pulling that video from your YouTube channel before it gets any more hits."

"What?" Elle said. "That's not right. I thought your deal was gone if I quit the label. Not if the label decided to cut me."

"Explain," Tommy said.

"I'd rather not discuss it," Elle said. "I'm sorry."

"And that answer speaks volumes," Webb said. "Does your father have anything to do with this?"

"Like I said, I'd rather not discuss it," Elle said again.

"Another answer that speaks volumes." Webb turned to Tommy. "I wondered about that. First you get a message from the top to give me a deal. Then you get a message that says my deal depends on her deal."

Webb turned back to Elle. "I'm going to ask you a question. An important question. At least, to me. I need to know if I was signed because of my music or because I am your friend. Did you have anything to do with your dad making me the offer? And don't say you'd rather not talk about it. We're friends. Or I thought we were."

"We are," Elle said. "And I didn't know about it. I was as surprised and happy about it as you were."

"Did you know that my deal depended on your deal?"

"Not until after it was done," Elle said. "At that point, it didn't seem like something I should tell you."

Webb stood, his fists clenched.

Tommy said to Webb, "You can't hold that against her."

"I know," Webb said, his back to both of them. "Still doesn't change how I feel about the situation."

"I can pull the video," Elle said.

Webb turned. "How will that help? I'll always know that I got the deal because you made it happen. So I don't think so. I'd rather go indie."

"If she doesn't pull the video," Tommy said, "you both lose your deals. That advance money? It won't reach you. In the label's eyes, the two of you are a package deal. And they'll wonder how come I can't control either of you."

Elle said, "I'm tired of being pushed around."

Tommy smiled. It was a sad and weary smile, just like the one she'd seen the previous day when he told her about the body double. "Me too. So I've got an idea. Why don't I quit before they fire me? Then I can have some fun helping the two of you go indie. Last I checked, your YouTube video had a half million hits. I'm pretty sure we can build on that and enjoy the journey."

He gave a dramatic pause and grinned. "I know it, because on my way here I received an interesting phone call. Elle, someone wants to interview you, and I've asked her to meet us here."

He stood. "In fact, here she is. Right on time."

The woman who approached had shiny dark hair with a few strands of bright purple, and a radiant smile. To Elle, she seemed like the kind of person you could be yourself with the minute you met her.

Tommy made the introductions. "Webb, Charlene, meet Deborah Evans Price. *Billboard* magazine."

Elle took a deep breath. Deborah Evans Price didn't need an introduction. She was one of the most trusted and beloved music-industry writers.

Tommy continued, "Deb, this is Webb and Charlene, both up-and-coming talents and good friends of mine."

"Glad Tommy could get us together," Deborah said. "When the YouTube video went viral, I asked him to send me some of your music, and we watched the charts. Now as you can guess, we also watch the clicks. Because when it goes viral, chances are the songs will hit the charts next."

Deborah pulled out a pad of paper and pencil from her purse, along with a handheld recorder.

"Webb," she said, "Tommy sent me your music, and I love it too. But this interview has to go to Charlene. Don't get me wrong. I love the music and I love the guys and I love bro-country. But it's time the girls had their turn. And we might as well start with Charlene. Let's talk. I promise, when the interview gets published, you're going to love the results."

Twenty-Two

"**L**et's consider this a board meeting," Elle's father said. "Obviously, it's an important one, since I flew down for it on short notice. The way I like to do business is to first agree on all the facts. The real discussion, then, is how to interpret those facts and then what actions to take based on those interpretations."

Elle said nothing.

Her father was speaking from where he sat in a leather chair in the living room of her condo. She was sitting on the matching leather couch. Except, really, it wasn't her condo. She only stayed in it. It was her father's.

"Here are the facts then," her father continued. "A corporation that I created and own made a substantial investment in a label with the expectation that as an artist you would deliver a product for a return on that investment. This implicit and explicit agreement was broken by the artist—you—in such a way that the label was unable to continue working with the artist. And—"

"No." Elle was quiet but firm.

"No? You disagree with the facts?" Her father showed no emotional reaction. No doubt it was why he was so successful in business.

"No. First, I'm not interested in treating this like a board meeting. I am your daughter. One who needs a father, not an investor."

"But we can separate those two things. We put the numbers on the table and make them work."

"No. We are not going to separate them. I don't want an investor. I want a father. I want someone who will let me cry on his shoulder when I need to. I want someone who will listen to my doubts. I want someone who is not a machine."

She caught him glancing at his watch. She walked over and pulled his hand into hers.

He gave her a puzzled frown.

"I want to believe I'm more important to you than what time it is," she said. "So here's the big question. Am I right?"

SIGMUND BROUWER & CINDY MORGAN

"You are my daughter."

"And you're treating me like an investment. So I'm going to put it on the line. Take off your watch. Put your phone on the table. And go for a walk with me."

She paused. She hadn't planned this, but somehow it seemed right. If it took busking and living off noodles to do it, she was ready to walk away from her dad's money. "And if you don't want a daughter, keep looking at the time, hold on to your phone and head back to your private jet to make your next meeting."

*　*　*

Elle was grateful for the timing, because she knew Harley and Webb were busking on their corner on 2nd Avenue, across from Coyote Ugly. As always, a small crowd was gathered.

The walk to the corner with her father had taken only a few minutes.

"Is that...?" he said, raising his voice to be heard above the music.

"Harley Hays," Elle said. "Most people don't recognize him with his ballcap that low. And you remember Jim Webb? I told you how he met Harley when they were both busking."

"Couldn't forget that," her father said. "Webb saved me a lot of money."

"Guess how much money Harley and Webb might earn for a couple hours on this corner?" Elle answered her own question. "Forty, maybe fifty bucks. Not a good return on their investment of time, wouldn't you agree?"

Her father didn't answer. She glanced up. She caught him mouthing the words to the song, his right foot tapping the ground in time to the music.

She tugged on her father's shoulder until he gave her his attention, and she pulled him far enough down the street that they could talk without distraction.

"I know that you are successful in business because you care about results," Elle said. "It's all spreadsheets and numbers in black and white."

He nodded.

"Those two care about the music," Elle continued. "Not what it gets them. Labels get in the way of that. Harley knows it. This is his escape."

Her father nodded again.

"I care about the journey," Elle said. "I know you started from nothing and built your empire, and you want so much for me because of what you didn't have when I was your age. I love you. I love you for caring for me like that."

She put her hand on her father's arm. "But your success has taken away my chance to carve out my own destiny. I've got a condo and a car I didn't earn, and I didn't earn my chance with a label. So how can I ever feel good about the results when it wasn't my journey? I want what you had. A chance to make it on my own and a chance to fail by myself."

"Do you have any idea how much I put into the label?"

"Do you have any idea how much that sounds like blackmail?" She smiled to take away the sting. "Besides, I doubt you put a cent into the label without looking at the numbers and deciding it would pay you back with or without my involvement as an artist."

It took a while, but he smiled in return.

"Fair enough," he said. He let out a deep breath. "You don't owe me anything in terms of the label.

But if you go indie, you pay rent on the condo. I take back the car. You're on your own financially."

"I'm okay with that," Elle said. "More than okay. I can't afford the condo, so I'll find my own place. I might even get roommates to share the rent. I can wait tables. I can busk. I don't care about the money. What I want is you there as a father. A father who can give me business advice when I ask."

Another long pause. Then her father said, "I'm okay with that too."

Elle swallowed hard. "You'll never know how much that means to me." She patted his arm. "I do have a big favor to ask though."

"What's that?"

"I want you to watch my next concert."

"Sure," he said.

"Great," Elle answered. "Follow me back to Harley and Webb, and if you like, you can throw a few bucks into the guitar case after I've finished."

She led her father back to the street corner and waved to get Webb's attention. His return grin was pure high voltage, and he waved her to join them.

After she pushed through the people in front, Harley gave her a high five and said, "Elle, I hear you've got a new song. Good thing Webb knows the chords. Ready to belt it out for us?"

"Call me Charlene," she said. "And yes, I'd love to sing it for you."

Acknowledgments

Big thanks to Sarah Harvey and Andrew Wooldridge for allowing me to be a part of this book. Thank you to Sigmund for being a splendid co-author. Thanks to my dear friend Deborah Evans Price, who continues to be such an amazing example of the kind of wonderful people that work in the music business. —CM

Bigger thanks to Cindy for using her amazing writing and storytelling skills to bring the Nashville music scene to life. —SB

SIGMUND BROUWER writes for both children and adults. In his popular presentations to young readers, Sigmund often plays the guitar (very badly). Sigmund and his family live half the year in Nashville, Tennessee, and half the year in Red Deer, Alberta. For more information, visit www.rockandrollliteracy.com.

CINDY MORGAN is an award-winning singer-songwriter based in Nashville, Tennessee, where she lives with her husband, Sigmund Brouwer, and their two daughters. Cindy's latest album, *Bows and Arrows*, and her memoir, *How Could I Ask for More*, were both released in 2015. For more information, visit www.cindymorganmusic.com.

To hear some of the songs from *Billboard Express*, and to learn how your teachers can invite Cindy or Sigmund to visit your school, please visit www.cindymorganmusic.com or www.sigmundbrouwer.com.

9781459804555 PB
9781459804562 PDF • 9781459804579 EPUB

Jim Webb believes that if you want to reach your
dreams, you have to live life loud. Bring the roof
down. Rock the boat. Make sure that when you
look back, you have no regrets. But when a shady
music producer steals one of Webb's songs, Webb
finds out how hard it is for a kid on his own
in Nashville to get justice. With the help of an
unlikely ally, Webb discovers that he has what it
takes to succeed: talent, determination and some
good friends.